International World
Peace Message

Meow Now

No Death, Only Transcendence

CODY "FLYING EAGLE" TEMPLETON

Gotham Books

30 N Gould St.
Ste. 20820, Sheridan, WY 82801
https://gothambooksinc.com/

Phone: 1 (307) 464-7800

© 2024 *Cody "Flying Eagle" Templeton*. All rights reserved.

No part of this book may be reproduced, stored in a retrieval system, or transmitted by any means without the written permission of the author.

Published by Gotham Books (October 5, 2024)

ISBN: 979-8-88775-797-1 (P)
ISBN: 979-8-88775-798-8 (E)

Because of the dynamic nature of the Internet, any web addresses or links contained in this book may have changed since publication and may no longer be valid.

The views expressed in this work are solely those of the author and do not necessarily reflect the views of the publisher, and the publisher hereby disclaims any responsibility for them.

Table of Contents

Introduction iv
Chapter 1 1
Chapter 2 5
Chapter 3 8
Chapter 4 12
Chapter 5 15
Chapter 6 17
Chapter 7 19
Chapter 8 21
Chapter 9 24
Chapter 10 26
Chapter 11 28
Chapter 12 30
Chapter 13 32
Chapter 14 34
Chapter 15 36
Chapter 16 39
Chapter 17 42
Chapter 18 44
Chapter 19 47
Chapter 20 49
Chapter 21 51
Chapter 22 53
Chapter 23 55
Chapter 24 57
Chapter 25 60
Chapter 26 62
"Meow Now" 65

INTRODUCTION

Luke Clear Eagle Lovesen called out to heaven. Great Father Sky who is opening his Ultimate Divine Dance. The first center is found between his legs, an energy center in the lower hips. He opens energy as he roots positively to Great Mother Earth. He opens his first energy center as he is connecting to Great Mother Earth. He is rooting in a kind spiritual healthy lifestyle, creating a new life.

Above the first energy center of the core, he raises divine energy as he connects to his masculine and feminine energy deep inside his second center. The second energy center is found to be at the base of the spine. The color of his second energy is orange.

He is joined by a loving angel Lea White Dove Lovesen in "Tree of Life" dance. She is openly and willing connecting to her 1st center and roots to the Great Mother Earth. Her roots are also red in color. Lea White Dove Lovesen is grounding to the core of Great Mother Earth.

Lea White Dove Lovesen raises her positive energy to the second center. Meow Now is a calling to her true self. She is joined her golden white light angel. Together two angels connect at two energy centers joined as one. Luke Clear Eagle Lovesen and Lea White Dove Lovesen are the peace dancers who share a spiritual path. Nitra -Girl cat calls again. Meow now for World Peace. They are allowed to dance internally by Great Mother Earth. I am dancing a sacred spiral of masculine and feminine energy.

In 2023, America has a strong reputation. Mankind needs an intramural dance. Peace Dancers know your purpose. Peace Dancers are encouraged to open the wisdom of your power animal. Become innocent as you dance. Your music and movement are an untold meditation. In this dance, Luke Clear Eagle Lovesen checks into his rhythm as well as his timing as he controls his breath. Breath is one energy life force that is the oneness with the universe.

Meow Now: No Death, Only Transcendence

Lea White Dove Lovesen's love is the feminine inspiration housing the energy needed to protect energy in a dance of the light. Two significant teachers offer divine dance as a way of wisdom. Peace dancing is balance life in the city of Sarasota Florida. Practice balancing daily is an energy dance of life.

The opening is parting the prayer hands, a symbol of expansion. Luke Clear Eagle Lovesen is chanting the way of compassion. Starting a new school of enlightenment. Dancing for world peace this year. Meow Now.

Chapter 1

"Om Mani Padme Hung" is a sound chant deep inside the core of nine centers of oneself. The "Peace Dancer" relates to the "Ra" soul. Any person may become a "Peace Dancer". "Meow Now," sings Nitra-Girl Cat. A "Peace Dancer", comes from the ultimate energy at the beginning of their life. In the beginning, a spirit body enters a physical body, opening the mental body, and sensing balance of the emotional body while feeling compassion. The "Peace Dancer" is a person of compassionate love, they become the Golden White Yellow Light of their spirit body.

The Peace Dancer reaches upward towards Great Father Sky's Spirit, with open prayer hands, as a connection is formed in the East, a space beyond the life of humans.

Luke Clear Eagle Lovesen relaxes as he opens his "Heart Energy" center with loving prayers. He places prayer hands over his "Heart Energy" center in his chest, as he begins his new breath of transcendence, then raises his prayer hands and opens his eastern view of clear blue space.

Every January 12th, on World Peace Day, Luke expands his view of life. Being a "Divine Peace Dancer", he brings his prayer hands together, and closes his prayer to Great Father Sky as he gathers unlimited wisdom.

Chanting "Om Ah Hung" a chant of understanding, a peaceful energy dancer inside himself, Luke Clear Eagle Lovesen knows the truth in performing his sacred spiral dance in all the nine known energy centers. He is a sacred person and transcends beyond his physical body and mental body. Breathing out with a controlled breath, he soothed his emotional body and felt bliss. He inhaled a deep breath, and collected the wisdom of everlasting life, then he exhaled the lies he was taught in childhood, in America. Luke Clear Eagle Lovesen sees with clear eyes, hears with clear ears, feels with increased sensation, and even tastes sensitive truth.

"Meow Now" says Nitra-Girl Cat.

He lowered his spiral dancing hands, and opened his hands to honor Great Mother Earth, thanking her for allowing him to stand and walk, and even dance a Divine Dance on Her today. When breathing in, Luke Clear Eagle Lovesen becomes a clear golden white yellow light spirit. He is aware of his power animal guide, the eagle, (a powerful symbolic bird of America), as it reminds him of the rights of the American people which could be expressed as "Ultimate Energy Dancers".

All "Peace Dancers" know the same hidden truth, held in a sacred spiral dance. Humankind shares one spirit, one Universal Golden White Light is who these peace dancers are. A Golden White Clear Light in the individual physical bodies.

Now in 2023, Luke takes note of his mental balance, along with his emotional confusion well as the causes of confusion. He takes a breathing check. He breathes in peace . As a peace dancer, he becomes a dancer after a war of thought patterns was programmed. Producing an idea that they are either masculine or feminine dancers. Either hot or cold, external or internal. Life is movement, and death is without movement. Therefore, when a peace dancer is ill, they must take a deep breath, hold it, release it, and breathe out slowly. This energy is deep and uses three levels of the lungs. Keep moving in a thoughtful moving, positive meditation as he brings his hands together, he raising his hands, and internal energy from up the earth. Nestling his prayer hands over his Heart Energy Center the house of emotions.

Luke Clear Eagle Lovesen is now connected to heaven in the astral dimension and earth is a third dimension of divine Golden White Yellow Light, as one positive peace dancer. He holds universal love energy from heaven. As he a Golden White yellow Light. He is consciously aware of spirit light of purple, along with all shades of purple, are remembered. Luke Clear Eagle Lovesen is joined this day by Lea White Dove Lovesen. The couple internally dance under a Tree of Life. He opens his eyes to witness to a field of Grouse dancing with an energy of sacred spiral of life. Glorious Grouse are inspiring all human peace dancers to do the same. Dancers awaken *their self-consciousness. Positive brainwaves in conscious thoughts.*

A nature of Golden White Yellow Light. The healing brainwaves of love become strong with daily practice become stronger. They are "Peace Dancers". They are dancing under the "Sacred Tree of Life", on a sacred path. His prayer hands gather over his "Heart Center" under the balanced beating of a healthy and well heart and offer good thoughts. Joyous brainwaves are housed with Golden White Light. The blood circulation is balanced with a strong immune system and he feels a healthy small intestine He expands a Purple colored light. A ball of light energy facing the east direction. His self-consciousness expands as a colored light 6 feet around him in 8 directions. His hands extend from his heart center as he holds positive thoughts for his loving partner Lea White Dove Lovesen. Breathing out he opens his hands, life energy is given power. His sacred spiral dance of life. Extending from his heart center he extends his hands to his sides. He turns his healing palms to Great Mother Earth. He lowers his healing hands to his sides as he bows to Mother Nature in respect. He lowers his healing palms to his sides.

Wisdom teachers have taught that our true father is Great Father Sky. Our true mother is Great Mother Earth, rooting and grounding us. Allowing us to journey on her daily. "Hey, yah ho". The music chants on the Cd player.

Luke Clear Eagle Lovesen's truth, a career, to gather divine energy then channel his divine Ra energy between Great Mother Earth and Great Father Sky. Great Mother Earth has everything we as people need to survive as we live our life. He lowers his hands to the planet Earth and gathers great mothers' gifts. The Great Mother Earth allows him to dance upon her. She is creating food and medicine in a rhythm of life. His cat is now comfortable in a rainbow light of loving trust.

Nitra-Girl Cat teaches him to receive the words of what to do. He is sensing the wisdom lesson of movement. Meditation is a dance guiding one deeper inside themselves.

Luke Clear Eagle Lovesen is preparing to take flight in his eagle spirit. His true spirit self is dancing in a 4/4 timing with Lea White Dove Lovesen who is dancing a soul connection to another place of the same mother earth. Lea White Dove Lovesen shares a spirit Divine Dance of light with Luke Clear Eagle Lovesen. Reaching everlasting heights, the Spirit Dancers dance in the heavens of clear blue light. World Peace is the gift for a troubled America.

Chapter 2

Immortal vigilante grew in new heights this year as the bird clan teaches. In the sacred spiral dancing a system, connects "Ra" energy our divine source to every movement in balanced harmony. Birds dancing in the sky of blue are considered the people of the sky. The sky people of this year build their home among the standing people, the tree people. Nitra-Girl Cat is nestled in the northeast direction. Lea White Dove Lovesen is here with her true power.

She is a "White Dove", she is in her power animal energy, she may hesitate. Along her pathway over 20 years ago when a failed marriage nearly ruined her. In the year 1995, life with creative deficiency disorder was difficult.

Lea White Dove Lovesen sought external ways of healing. She turned to other free white doves. She went deeper in prayer and dance to balance her life. Her life now is harmony in and balanced energy. She loves a kind healing angel. Luke Clear Eagle Lovesen is a "Flying Eagle" by nature. He is Golden White Yellow Light. He granted her freedom to be herself. Luke Clear Eagle Lovesen allowed himself to trust and love her openly. This action is something he has taken for the first time in this human body. The year 2023 marks a time of protecting the energy of "Ra" light. A vibration of Golden White Yellow Light.

"Ra" light is mankind's life source. Lea White Dove Lovesen and Luke Clear Eagle Lovesen are partners in life living as "Ra" were teaching at different locations, at the same time of day, every 12th of January. In one Peace Dance as one Dancer.

They are the same "Noble truth". These truths are known as the 4 noble truths in sacred internal dance simultaneously. The sense of hearing music and commandments Divine Dance became observed. Seeing the Golden White Yellow Light of people happens becomes a moving meditation. Spiritual consciousness is created by a breath of life. The expressive color of clarity found in a "Baby Dragon" opens consciousness of the purple spirit and is at the height of direct understanding. They are connecting as a "Ra" Goddess. Peace dancers open their divine selves, in one moving spirit of self-clarity.

Luke Clear Eagle Lovesen connected to Lea White Dove Lovesen. She is connected to Luke Clear Eagle Lovesen. Their sacred spiral is shield formed alongside Astel the Armadillo. They are shielded today in a sacred spiral dance of harmony led by Cleo the Field Grouse medicine of the heavens. Protecting diverse energy is needed today for world peace. A balanced dance of masculine and feminine energy. Lea White Dove Lovesen and Luke Clear Eagle Lovesen are one energy. The dancers see one another, hear one another, and even feel one another.

The lovers join one another in tasting the of taste. A taste of filtered water. Lea White Dove Lovesen the medicine White Dove power animal hesitated. Along her pathway over 20 years ago when a failed marriage ruined her 1995 life with creative deficiency. Lea White Dove Lovesen sought external ways of healing. She turned to prayer and internal meditative dance to balance her life. In her life now she loved the kind healing of an angel Luke Clear Eagle Lovesen. He is a Flying Eagle. He granted her freedom. Luke Clear Eagle Lovesen allows himself to trust and love her openly. He danced in a divine internal dance meditation.

2023 marked a time of protecting the energy of "Ra" light. "Ra" light is mankind's life source. Lea White Dove Lovesen and Luke Clear Eagle Lovesen were teaching at different locations, at the same time of day, every 12th of January. In one Dance as one Dancer.

They simultaneously shared the same noble truths, known as the 4 noble truths. A sacred internal dance. Their divine dance becomes observed. A moving meditation, with spiritual consciousness and controlled with breath.

The expressive color consciousness of purple is a height of direct connecting. A peaceful dancer with their divine self, in a moving spirit of self-clarity. The dancers are the same spirit.

    Luke Clear Eagle Lovesen is connected to Lea White Dove Lovesen. In a sacred spiral dance of harmony. Protecting diverse energy now is needed today for world peace. A balanced dance of masculine and feminine energy. Lea White Dove Lovesen and Luke Clear Eagle Lovesen are one energy. The dancers see one another, hear one another, and even feel one another. The lovers join one another in tasting the clear taste of filtered water. Cursive thought brainwaves are a team project. This team shares the vibration of life, tantra love. "Sacred Peace Dance".

    The sacred dance is possible through the Divine Dancers. Emptying cursive brainwaves. Emptying ego. Luke Clear Eagle Lovesen is trained in the wisdom of Buddhism and Zen. No death only transcendence.

    Today he clears his mind of thinking. His blood moves together with her inside, his heart organ. He is working on a concept of a certain Lea White Dove Lovesen. Everything he sees is based on a particular concept his best friend becomes when she is with him as one soul self. He doesn't see her solid self. He is filled with his best friend's soul self. He is filled with her unconditional love. Her masked self is a concept of his material world thinking. Her beautiful body is based on his concepts and experiences. This is the projection of his ego. A trained behavior today.

    Lea White Dove Lovesen is in truth, much more than his ego perception. She is a spirit of clear purple and gold light. As shared by Cleo the field Grouse, is an ultimate never-ending loving energy in a dance of life.

    The aforementioned becomes a trusted truth they share. In two complete Physical bodies along with two mental bodies. This couple shares an expanded life as ultimate energy dancers, a lifestyle.

Chapter 3

Another beautiful slightly breezy day in Florida. The current day temperature is 69 degrees cool. Studying nature here on every 12th day of January. The time has come to increase the combination of movement as a meditation.

Have positive forward thinking. Lea White Dove Lovesen and Luke Clear Eagle Lovesen program particular movements to be within the physical skin housing their life force. Directing the cells of humankind.

Directing controlled breathing patterns to the sacred spiral of the double helix of selfishness is DNA. A property of energy. "Peace Dancers" program their mind to create peace through thoughts.

A positive and negative system of divine dance begins in the positive nature of not only Lea White Dove Lovesen and Luke Clear Eagle Lovesen. But of all of humankind as they perform their sacred movements.

Nitra-Girl Cat a temple cat watched as Cleo the Field Grouse spiraled in the clouds of light. The ultimate energy dance frees the people of America through the coiled effect of a self-analyzed time and rhythm.

People, students, and dancers of music, and movement. Meditators finds their light is who they are. Light Dancers in clear white light are not afraid of death. They see as well as understand death as a concept of experiencing a certain daily dance, in many forms of passion or compassion housed in a solid body, mental body, and emotional body as a spiritual body.

People are Peace entering the human form unite in a spiritual light and power animal.

Lea White Dove Lovesen the power animal hesitated. Along her pathway over 20 years ago when a failed hardship lifestyle ruined her in 1995. She began a new life by starting with creative deficiency. Lea White Dove Lovesen sought external ways of healing. She turned to prayer and dance to balance her life. Her life now she loved a kind healing angel.

Luke Clear Eagle Lovesen is a Flying Eagle. He granted her freedom. Luke Clear Eagle Lovesen allowed himself to trust and love her openly. This year marked a time of protecting the energy of " Ra" Light. "Ra" Light is mankind's life source. Lea White Dove Lovesen and Luke Clear Eagle Lovesen was teaching at different locations, at the same time of day, on every 12th of January, in one Dance as one Dancer.

They shared the same noble truths, known as the four noble truths in sacred internal dance simultaneously. A divine dance was observed. A moving meditation, with spiritual consciousness and breath. The expressive color consciousness is purple a height of direct connecting, a Peace Dancer with their divine self, in a moving spirit of self-clarity.

Luke Clear Eagle Lovesen connected to Lea White Dove Lovesen in a sacred spiral dance of harmony. Protecting diverse energy is needed today for world peace. A balanced dance of male and female energy. Lea White Dove Lovesen and Luke Clear Eagle Lovesen are one energy. The dancers see one another, hear one another, and even feel one another. The lovers join one another in tasting the clear taste of filtered water. Cursive thought patterns that creates a positive brainwave.

As Americans, it is time to dance internally with one another. A person opening their Divine Self. This is an invitation from "Cleo the Field Grouse". A time to dance inside with the spiritual medicine of healing compassion. The divine "Child of the North" internal dance in eight directions. Soon this divine child will grow to be a divine "Adolescent of the South".

"Ultimate Energy Dance" is a "Spiritual Dance" of light energy in all eight directions. Thank you for turning on your spiritual self. The Light being you are. Your Spirit is one "Ra" Spirit self. Starting as a conduit of energy between Heaven, Great Father Sky, and Great Mother Earth. Our planet Great Mother Earth is not flat. You, "Peace Dancers" of light, are clear and sacred. You are Granter all good things to be the energy of wisdom between your Great Mother Earth and Great Father Sky. One Nation of "Peace Dancers" united on

World Peace Day. Peace is set in motion. The analyzed action of our truth and why we are here for world peace and healing.

When dancing the sacred spiral divine dance, it is important not to force a projected will on another dancer of peace. For Example: Forcing COVID or any microbial disease on another "Peace Dancer" was known as chemical warfare predicted back in the time of 60's. An internal "Peace Dancer" is led by the breath. "Peace Dancing" is controlled breathing. A pattern enlightening our mind's wisdom. Exposing our lying society.

The American Bald Eagle taught about chemical medicine. Its effects in 2023 the medical profession taught pharmacists and forced toxic drugs on a person. That means against their will. This action acts as a tyranny.

This is not freedom.

Luke Clear Eagle Lovesen is the son of several teachers a well-known lesson revisited is "No" means "No" when someone says "No". The need for education by teachers of the "Mountain Lion Clan" is to back off, and stop pushing their way.

Legally this means the action of mentally placing "guilt" on a person is not accepted. Wellness is a way of life, entering this year. "Peace Dancers" dance for peace unite. Dance on into this year.

Lea White Dove Lovesen, a White Dove power animal became hesitated, along her pathway over 20 years ago when a failed marriage ruined her in 1995. Her life changed and became a lifestyle of creative deficiency. Lea White Dove Lovesen sought external ways of healing. She turned to prayer and dance to balance her life. Her life now she loved a kind healing angel Luke Clear Eagle Lovesen. He is a Flying Eagle. He granted her freedom. Luke Clear Eagle Lovesen allowed himself to trust and love her openly. 2023 marked a time of protecting the energy of "Ra" Light. "Ra" light is mankind's life source. Lea White Dove Lovesen and Luke Clear Eagle Lovesen were teaching at different locations, at the same time of day, every 12th of January.

In one "Peace Dance" as one "Peace Dancer". They shared the same noble truths. These truths are simultaneously known as the four noble truths in sacred internal dance. A divine dance was observed. A moving meditation, with spiritual consciousness and breath. The expressive color consciousness of purple is a height of direct connecting a Dove Peace dancer with their divine self, in a moving spirit of self-clarity.

Luke Clear Eagle Lovesen connected to Lea White Dove Lovesen in a sacred spiral dance of harmony. Protective diverse energy is needed today for world peace. A balanced dance of masculine and feminine energy. Lea White Dove Lovesen and Luke Clear Eagle Lovesen choose to become one energy. The "Peace Dancers" see one another, hear one another, and even feel one another as one in spirit.

The lovers join one another in tasting an unmistakable taste of filtered water. Cursive brainwave thoughts are washed away. Healing brainwaves inside their divine dance, become clearer. The root center asks our Great Mother Earth Gaia. permission to dance upon her the gift giver. Gaia grants permission to the "Peace Dancer" and the energy of gravity holds them to the Great Mother Earth.

Chapter 4

The reputation of this year, tell me your story, "Peace Dancers"—dance together as one person. Even hold a Tai Chi Dance Fan of defense or a walking stick. A wooden flute may stop a battle or an argument before it starts.

Tell me the story. If you have told Luke Clear Eagle Lovesen along with Lea White Dove Lovesen to express a story of their souls' life inside two different material bodies. They will know well creating healing now starts with a cleanse. Clean the exterior physical body. The house where the soul lives and the roots of the energy core consciousness awakens the peace dancer to the true self. Their soul turning the core to the right, the peace dancer opens feminine self-consciousness, known as soul work.

Freeing what entraps a peaceful dancer, separates them from karma in 2022.

Now in this year, Lea White Dove Lovesen, teaches a fan MMM Dance of Defense along with MMM music, movement, and meditation to 5 rooted peace dancers of the morning.

The practice cleansings the frustrated mind. Dancers flock on every 12th of January, to her for the cleansing and more, moving meditation. Before the traditional ways of China, were the ways Tibet performed. As a breath-controlled exercise of Lung and Large Intestine energy pathways feeding of the core center of Golden White Yellow Light.

Her ability to assist in helping the mind, the body as well as the emotional ego connects to the divine soul. Working with breath along with connection and restoration. "Peace Dancers", souls connect to her soul to her as a teacher and trainer, being respectful a key keyword in power training. "Peace Dancers" face the powerful direction of the East as they dance the "Divine Child of the North" internal dance. An internal divine dance internally, telling their soulmates, a story of their love in rainbow light restores balance. This is a time to live in your truth. Your character may be misinformed as to your power and who you are.

Do you have a reputation? "Peace Dancers" have a nature. Tell me your truth. It is ok if you don't. "Peace Dancers" inside the house is known as the material body, for the soul's light appears, it is translated as the nine sacred centers. In the Ultimate Energy dancing, masculine and feminine are housed in the nine houses. The first house is the nature of self-intact. Consistent in who the "Peace Dancers" personality is formed and held in their life who they are as they dance on. Any day of this year.

Lea White Dove Lovesen is designed by her truth. She experiences her truth by experiencing Music, Movement as a Moving Meditation MMM. Actions for discovering truth and her true self. She is coming to find she, not her physical body, a rainbow of light, creating a flow of energy. The energy paths of her true light are clear, expanding outward, three feet in all creating her Purple Aura of Grand Ma the one who reaches "Peace Dancers" to find theirs.

Ultimate soul dancers of world peace meet in the light of Ra the sacred dance of the soul in the root center of the material body. Lea White Dove Lovesen trains daily and teaches weekly. Her soulmate Luke Clear Eagle Lovesen this year is dancing as a transformed self. An Ultimate Energy Dance. Breathe in as you begin to expand yourself, filling the three levels of your lungs with air and essential oil mist. Balance the root center and raise your prayer hands to Great Father Sky in tune with the balance dissolving the ego self-created by your mind and your thinking self.

Come as you Luke Clear Eagle Lovesen and Lea White Dove Lovesen have physical selves. You both create the third self with a root center from heaven where you both return to in time. The Spirit is your true self and returns to heaven. Your material body naturally returns to Great Mother Earth and there is no death only transformation to light.

"Peace Dancers" change the vibration frequency as they dance the pulsating dance. Luke Clear Eagle Lovesen feels like one person in a waltz of love and peace. In 4x4 time as he breathes in, he holds, in harmony with Lea White Dove

Lovesen, which is his feminine nature she is the creation of love, a light in a sacred spirit union. Her MMM Dance is internally connecting at the root center with herself. This action is bliss, a form of protection and expansion. Thank you, Great Mother Earth. Luke Clear Eagle Lovesen looks across the miles. He is in a portal of purple light blending his light with Lea White Dove Lovesen, his angelic self, his light. He is her light and he free himself in a unifying action unites connecting to her purple light self in a Tantra union, heaven. This bright radiant being is real. Meow Now.

The root is a union of who they are, in light bodies. His masculine nature is in harmonious connection with the divine masculine Lea White Dove Lovesen. Transformation to the Golden White Yellow Light within her dance. She becomes her truth in teaching loving children.

Chapter 5

In protection and creation, Luke Clear Eagle Lovesen and Lea White Dove Lovesen hold the colors of the rainbows. The colors of a rainbow light. Every time they dance their forms hold sunyata in space. Others may know them as empty. This is what they want. The divine energy form dances on sacred mother earth. Together their material life is united turning into one unified root center. Their spirit rises in a Purple Clear White Light. Spinning a Purple Clear White Light in the 2nd center. The crystal-clear physical form appears as a solid body yet this form is not who they are. They are the lights, of the rainbow formed after a rainstorm. A Purple Clear White Light appears in the space 6 feet all around them.

In all directions, this center is spinning a Purple Clear White Light raising and opening the second energy center energy at the base of the spine. The sexual center is orange in color and clearly held in the second center is sexual center spiraling a Purple and Clear creative light balancing the action of the design producing peace. The "Peace Dancer" maintains loving passion just below the sacrum in the hips. In the core center. The life force energy is the sacred center of the hips, a sign of sexual passion. Uniting their sexual desire, a red light ignites the colors of white as well as purple and shades of violet. Uniting excites a handsome man and beautiful woman in physical form as the red light of fiery passion, causes a climax of delight. Entering the purple, white light of Divine Joy. They find they have nothing to lose in love, in the "Ultimate Dance of Love". Each ultimate energy dancer is one, healing past issues they find they own and form their hardship on a spiritual plane. How they perceive the joy they experience is the action of their mind form. Their mental body.

Thinking is the joy of understanding. Joy is a freeing emotion. Honoring each other is a joy of breathing in each other, the energy of passion their light body dance, and filing their material body with universal oneness. Their passion rises. This joy is experienced in 8 directions of MMM. "Meow Now" says Nitra-Girl Cat.

Information is the powerful Golden White Yellow Light they hold in the third center. The third center unwinds and unfolds hidden truth. Balancing the distance of form, the couple dances a sacred internal dance of the third center. The gift is all good things come to them. Their light attracts others of divine light. Bring spiritual healing to an ill and diseased society. "Meow Now".

In this time, a new lifestyle culture begins, as the way of baby boomers' culture fades away along with the reputation of being misinterpreted. A new year with four new bodies is in bloom.

Chapter 6

 A clean digestion system is a task to be created in the belly of anyone seeking peace. A Center for Rappelling. This is the yellow light of a rainbow held at the third center. How does Lea White Dove Lovesen' and Luke Clear Eagle Lovesen uphold the truth in a harmonious energy dance using the color yellow, dominating the third center. The center is stimulated by unconditional love. Forming a space at the third center in the solar plexus. The "Peace Dancer" becomes one golden light of truth. One divine true love has several different experiences in this time of intuition. Keep the golden light shining through a rainbow of light. Is the Angelic work found concerning a daily exercise, an undertaking taken daily? "Peace Dancers" learn to dissolve the trauma from a created ego. The tone of the voice and facial codes is how a peaceful dancer says, "May all good things come to you". "Meow Now".

 Could the sound mean that a "Peace Dancer" is either a light of love and attracts other light workers in a Peace Dance is repelling what is untrue, not to be trusted? The task daily for lightworkers is to join others and gain respect, along with self-loving, dissolving ego transforming to their soul in golden light. Giving a gift becomes the movement of energy internally in the sacred spiral found in wave hands like clouds. Loving and respecting their soul self is an action of attitude. This action will attract others of like mind.

 Facing the west direction as the Sun descends in the afternoon hours. Luke Clear Eagle Lovesen and Nitra-Girl Cat, his faithful cat joined by his beloved angel Lea White Dove Lovesen to raise his self-esteem. He feels the soul connection as he sees her light a scent of peppermint comes to join his third center to her third center in light of peace. A clear Golden White Yellow Light dances in the palms of Lea White Dove Lovesen as she is joined by "Keen White Dove" the reincarnated granddaughter of a pink and white light. The positive energy of "Peace Dancer" is in the breath of the pink rainbow light. Beings in sacred self-esteem, raising and *lowering their hands becomes the action of Raising self-esteem. Listening to a positive ego self. Not all aspects of the ego are negative.*

Opening a positive aspect of a "Peace Dancer" on a journey. Life under a tree of life is needed to thrive. Nitra-Girl Cat becomes the leadership being taught this year. A year that opens with a divine energy dance of the "Divine Child of the North". This internal divine dance is righting what is a misconception attitude of the dance. Your dance is different. Dance forward in a strong scent of life. Choosing a scent you like to cleanse indifference. The result of this action stops the leakage of energy. Healing oneself. "Meow Now".

As Cleo the Field Grouse, the one feline animal who taught Nitra-Girl Cat who passes it on to Luke Clear Eagle Lovesen and Lea White Dove Lovesen. If your "Divine Dance" is not your best dance, your ego self is not in the material form it sticks and is not helping the others grow. (Chant) "Om Mani Pademe Hung" for compassion. Breathe in your essential oil which connects your centers in a spiral of energy. Repel what is not raising your vibration. Breathe in your 100% pure essential oil scent. "No Death Only Transformation".

Balance daily, becoming an "Aqua Blue Light" for "World Peace" Someone in the material world will see your glowing self. They will see your physical body and a smile will heal them.

No death only transformation of hardship into joy. A Purple White light of the spiritual self. Your true self. Dancing in balance harmony of spiritual light causes the ego self to manifest a spray repelling sent toward doctors and staff of false medicine. Meow Now.

Chapter 7

The yard is the home of many animals and many animal spirits. Opening a Divine Dance, innocence people become awakened. The energy of "Kleene the guardian angel" comes to Luke Clear Eagle Lovesen on this day of enlightenment. A Greenlight is turned on today. Setting Peace Dancers free in love. Friends become family. "World Peace" is an "RA" energy dance of innocence. A prayer of World Peace is offered from the internal fourth heart center, the heart center. A healthy innocent heart. Nitra-Girl Cat Offers a "Meow Now" comment. "Meow Now" is offered to Great Father Sky. An offering from a healthy fifth upper chest center. Balance in the immune system is a new concept today presented to the south direction. Please protect the children of our material world. As the "Peace Dancer" protects their child within themselves. Knowing when to trust this medicine and education. For a healthy immune system. The gentle, tentative child is the lesson of this green light in the south direction.

Lea White Dove Lovesen stays in timing. She became playful in life, under the "Tree of Life". From the "Tree of Life, children show respect not taught in homes and schools. Maintained in the music and harmonious movement, she discovered in her quiet meditation time on the fourth and fifth centers. The heart and immune system centers.

This practice of MMM and Ultimate Energy Dance Dancer balances the center of life with understanding a reason to love innocently. A very powerful medicine of trust. A loyalty toward belief in the treatment of a gentle porcupine. Understanding Great Mother Earth and "Kleene the guardian angel" is a way of enlightenment. The power to change schools and health care this year. Trusting the source in which a child is created. A "Peace Dancer" is born again, learns to trust oneself by listening to messages of God and Goddess. The "Peace Dancers" united in perfect harmony inside the core of our physical self.

The challenge is not to lose connection to the divine self. The light color of green is a color of a great mystery. Is it possible that this trust in innocence may open energy portals of divine light in people of all ages? Trust is sharing love, becoming joyous. Knowing you are not alone in a "Greenlight Portal of Love".

"Kleene is a guardian angel, a Holder of Innocents" when she feels unsafe, she spread her sharp quills of protection. Porcupine wisdom. Lea White Dove Lovesen has a Golden White Yellow Light while she teaches the ways of truth. She becomes a teacher and is beginning to ask, "Why do her bosses wish her to stop teaching?" She brings people joy to the internal dance a to her students. Class numbers increase and while she collapses her sharp quills. She spread her quills when she is misunderstood. She poses a threat because she has a superior approach of teaching compared to school teachers or everyday people.

Misunderstood like Cleo the Skunk the holder of reputation. She sprays a stink when threatened. Luke Clear Eagle Lovesen is a keeper of the color clear. He is misinterpreted and banished for his protection. In anger now, this year. Is he still outside a society of clicks or is he still held as a threat?

Judgments this year go against the rainbow green light held at the chest center. People of this year must learn respect in society and shine a green light on the children of this year. Be playful and have fun in life. Know when to spray the scent or display the quills. As your Spiritual Guide speaks to him every day, he finds balance as he internally dances "RA Divine Energy Dances" in the Great Mystery. Meow Now.

Chapter 8

To all "Peace Dancers" in this year, the fourth, fifth, and sixth energy center when a Peace Dancer dies, the soul or spirit is the true self. The true self is set free, and as the life in internal dance is finished, Divine Dance is experience. The Divine Dance is an internal mental and emotional program. Death means a transformation to a light Body of rainbow colors, this is a skill achieved in material form. "No death only transcendence".

Luke Clear Eagle Lovesen is dancing on a rainbow with Lea White Dove Lovesen. This loving energy couple is one clear golden-yellow rainbow light. The practice of this skill in one spirit self is known as Tantra Energy Oneness. Energy light returns as their one true self. Free from a physical form. Free of unclear mental misinterpretations of life. The color of life glows in a teal aura and nine centers of a material form. "Peace Dancers" breathe air and drink water, and ingest life-sustaining foods.

Energy in the movement of their dance. Becomes a re-framed lifestyle, a positive life. Balance is a Peace Dancer's spiritual self. Power inside the centers of material form is produced. These centers root, as they move in a trusted dance of life.

The spinning of the masculine and feminine centers in an energy dance as one person is comforting the wounded "Peace Dancer". The Golden White Yellow Light of their aura shines brighter. Teaching the individual self to maintain consciousness in order to control self-confidence again. "Peace Dancers" holding this light at the fourth, fifth, and sixth centers of the material form unite people of peace. Peace is created on this day.

An ill-granted lifestyle may mean this is a day to spread the sharpness of our words. Anti-war, anti-chemical, war-anti false humans creating diseases like COVID. And the causes of COVID or angry children in schools with a weapon, who were taught it is okay to take aggression out on family and friends.

Pain to others is not funny. A peace dance "Divine Child of The North" is the chosen internal dance of Sunyata-Kai International.

This divine dance is designed to bring life power.

The divine is a daily defense to all Peace Dancers. "Peace Dancers" in this year aren't vulnerable under a "Ra" energy shield. "Peace Dancers" strengthen hope inside a physical body. One with the divine self-spinning nine energy centers in the core of light. Om Meow Now.

"Peace Dances" around the Great Mother Earth join in the light body as they share their prayers from their souls for world peace the action to stop the wars of the world now. accept a little love this day from others. Accept the ways of natural medicine as you breathe in the essential oil of Frankincense. Goddess' energy is awakening and consciousness in movements opens the door to trust in people of like mind.

What has a peace dancer learned since 1994 when the flying eagle appeared to him and 1st writing was a conviction toward world peace? A challenge for warriors to become dancers and stop fighting. Governments were teaching people that people were a material form of the human body. A baby boomer who are physical bodies where a divine soul lives. In this year, there is much common and it appears to peace dancers as enlightenment. A gift from Goddess. All humans are a soul living with a material body. Share your light as you join others in a heavenly belief. Trust in peace and with unconditional love. Honor Great Mother Earth. Take action to breathe in and direct your soul to root in the 1st center. The astronomical poles shifted in 1994. Each woman is a friend giving life to the new generations of life. No Death! "Peace Dancers" this year, have a new education process. Creating a transformation in new babies.

The world is a place for peace as new life means respect for life. Lea White Dove Lovesen speaks her truth... "Respect nurtures trust, bringing families back to respect in this year brings unconditional love of families". She adds "Working together as one light with rainbow colors of yellow and gold, a "Peace Dancer" is dancing inside to balance the 4th energy center". Every being knows this truth. Goddess brings gifts of daily peace. Peace inside, healing old wounds of peace dancers. Those children that has been from 1994 to 2022, ego must dissolve and allowing humble innocent child to lay, learn, and dance the ways of peace in harmony with honor toward mothers of babies, especially the created babies, and creative ways toward peace.

Jan 12 of this year, shines a rainbow of understanding and forgiving wayward children in ego ways because they were not taught a better life. The ways of transforming material bodies to light bodies means clearing a clouded confused mind along with finding joy in every movement in every Divine Dance. "Meow Now".

Take Time to love yourself.
Peace is a rhythm of kind actions.
Actions are the rewards Peace Dancers,
Moving meditation is a reward for loving-kindness.
Stillness is measured by internal consciousness.
Art of balancing, "No Death, only transformation to light".
Internal Dance creates a balance in the core of centers,
therefore, is not religion.

CHAPTER 9

"The Secret of Survival from Sammy the Squirrel"

    Opening the sixth center of the 9 centers of energy, the voice energy located in the throat, is a secret of survival. Lea White Dove Lovesen stands in a Chicago Park, facing the sky. She is opening the doors of her throat center, she stands, bringing masculine protective energy through her core uniting her core of rainbow light with her guardian angel. Rooting to Great Mother Earth her feminine self joins with Luke Clear Eagle Lovesen in a Spiritual Divine, Ultimate Internal Energy Dance. Her light body becomes freer as more light is produced in the second center. Thriving, her life energy raises to the 3rd center uniting in a cleaning nurturing Golden White Yellow Light. Any misinterpreted brainwave patterns become clear now.
    Her cat companion joins her on this fun day of Peace. Bella-Girl Cat is a black and white cat who sits in front of Lea White Dove Lovesen as she dances her divine dance. The attentive action brings a smile to passers-by. Her leadership lesson opens the understanding of Lea White Dove Lovesen. Not all tree cuttings are for burning, some cuttings make great shelters for her cat. Meow Now. Lea White Dove Lovesen is deep inside her sixth center. It is her perception of her feelings telling her to become clearer about her Om Meow says Bella-Girl Cat.
    Why does she do things in her simple life to create a response to her prieved self? To become clearer is goal. She breathes in through her nose and breath out through her mouth, a breath of frankincense essential oil. She feels a passion for spiritual life as she looks at her divine cat, Bella-Girl Cat.
    A smile comes over her face as a sense of joy comes to her, she moves her core to her left side. She hears "Sammy the Owl" call her from a tree. Teaching a Key to Survival. She senses the owl in the trees behind her right shoulder. The core energy

stirs the circulation of blood and energy. Turning her core to the left side, the camouflage changes as she sees the mother owl in the standing oak tree before her and her young one examining the way of "Kleene the innocent one", in harmony with each other. "World Peace Day" truly is today. Lea White Dove Lovesen is re-arranging her life as well as lifestyle. She is more aware of her feelings. Trusting there are balanced breaths in the air on a slight cool breeze. Lea White Dove Lovesen is moving her material body to the balance of right and left. She is balancing trust and faith.

She continues to raise her spirit light within her energy core. Her heart center which is the fourth center located in the chest, to her immune system center which is the fifth center, and upward to her voice center which is the sixth center located in the throat.

The same ways her ancestors have for thousands of years. The process is not easy in a system of emotional abuse. The causes of being misunderstood brings on defenses of porcupine medicine. Understanding her power is her task as a holder of light in a body of a higher vibration as well as a higher frequency. Her energy meridians are balanced and alive. The wisdom of Sammy the Owl flies on.

Chapter 10

"Amma the Dolphin," a sea mammal teaches the ways of breathing. A Florida Day is inviting "Peace Dancers" to share the ultimate energy of Atlantean ancestors. Peace is a "Ra" energy Internal Dance of mammals. Human as dolphins and whales share the same oxygen as humans and space keepers do. Breathing is not religion. Amma the Dolphin who is not a fish however is a Sea Mammal. People from all over Great Mother Earth witness the power of oxygen in a life dance with carbon dioxide. Human people have an experience with this power. A vital life-giving force. Lea White Dove Lovesen and Luke Clear Eagle Lovesen share space in life today. Every 12th of January, they dance with the Atlantean Goddess in material form and "Ra" energy.

"Peace Dancers" join the Divine Energy Dance of breathing. Inhalation focusing their thoughts in the root center while they visualizes a red ray of light from their legs and hips. Filling the core center with life-sustaining energy. Filling the three levels of lungs with oxygen as well as with 100% pure essential oils.

Lea White Dove Lovesen repeats this action three times awakening the self-consciousness in all 9 centers as she moves her prayer hands to her chest and her heart center. She feels compassion along with a love of innocence and bravery. She needs to expel the toxic gas of carbon dioxide, before her next inhalation. This is a breathing dance before movement begins.

Luke Clear Eagle Lovesen greets the same pure energy of the Great Spirit and Great Mother Earth igniting his compassion from his heart. The rhythm of the music is in tune with life. This is life's rhythm. "Peace Dancers" connect to the rhythm of life as well as their personal, individual rhythm. Healing divine energy begins. This energy grows. Anxiety is dissolved and emotions are resolved. A rhythm found in "Divine Aqua Energy Dance" moving through the water is really easy when the mind is clear.

Amma the Dolphin known as "Guru of breathing" taught the art of breathing as a life-sustaining art. She taught ocean breathing exercises. She is in a sacred balance between two gases of the air. She is in harmony as she plays and dances on the ocean waves. "Amma" is Dolphin energy. She is in tune with the energy of the universe. Breathing is a good energy exercise Air before Dancing internally with the "Divine Child of the North" or the "Divine Adolescent of the South".

Breathe in long and deep breaths. A Peace Dancer may find they lost count of the number or the movement they were on. Peace Dancers recover their thoughts and dance on. When a Peace Dancer forgets the order of movements they are the Peace transformed into one of the colors of the Rainbow. Is it possible to tell a story to the emotions or mentally telling the Peace Dancer what they need to perfect the Internal Dance? They are supported by the energy of the heavens activated by their divine self. In a rainbow light.

Nitra Girl says, Meow Now.

Chapter 11

Sammy the Owl shares Owl Oneness.

They may connect to the "Divine Child of the North" and "Adolescent of the South" in two divine internal energy dances. This combination is the divine growth and development of a human. Internally Peace Dancers share the energy of Sammy the Owl. The life force is present internally and is used to heal tired dancers. Release stagnant emotions within the movements. The atom of everyone who shares the harmony of today's Ultimate Energy Dance that is found in the nine centers. Keeping with rhythm of smooth jazz. Peace Bliss therapy for the dancer and all who seek World Peace. This is a dance internally inside. One with Great Spirit essence.

Following the ways of the Divine Dance, the life energy force is world peace utilizes full rich breaths. The cells of all dancers are revitalized with oxygen. The moon sister joins the dance as she reveals the patterns for life on the movements of life in internal breath-guided dance. This dimension breaks physical limitations and Peace Dancers join other Peaceful people in moving prayer and meditation. We urge people to dance a World Peace Dance in day dreamtime. Day Dreamtime is a space between two realities.

How many people shares World Peace? How many Peace Dancers as well as Peace Makers forget to breathe on World Peace Day on every 12th of January? Lea White Dove Lovesen or Luke Clear Eagle Lovesen shares a connected dance on this day. In dancing World Peace, the Peace Dancers dances internally, the chosen dance of World Peace. Today may bring consciousness of excess stress and the Peace Dancers have the opportunity to release the stress.

Old injuries both physical and mental may appear in night-time dreams. Make ready your dream catcher. Are you on a fast? Time to cleanse? Did you check your natural cycles? This the time to accept changes. Breathe in and with your breath out, dance the movement blocking World Peace. The

Internal Dance is a time of no death only transcendence. Like Dolphins, dance between water and sky. Sammy the Owl flies between Great Father Sky and Great Mother Earth. This is your light dancing on the waves of thoughts.

Old breath is hanging at the bottom of the lungs. A deep breath out releases an old breath and multiple patterns blocking our World Peace. Filling the lungs, peaceful dancers have to tame the wild animal as they let go of their ego ways, they lighten up. Peace is danced in a rainbow of light. The color from the heart radiating out is a green color light.

Luke Clear Eagle Lovesen joins with Lea White Dove Lovesen on this day of peace as they dance a heart-felt healing process of unconditional love. It is said and even written that when you pay close attention to how you feel, you are listening to Amma the Dolphin and Sammy the Owl, which is connected to you too.

The Peace Dancers are bringing regeneration to the lungs. Healing energy is for the third center (Solar Plexus) and fourth center (Heart Center), joining and sharing the spinning of these centers in balance. Joining and sharing the spinning of these centers. Uniting as one soul in everlasting love.

Divine World Peace Day Dance is focused on Internal Peace Dancers no matter what your style. The "Peace Dancers" way creates energy for world peace. If this is not happening, the "Peace Dancers" principles need to be looked at. Practice Internal Dance Daily. And share the green light of your heart center. Expanding six feet around you in every direction. This is the wisdom of Sammy the Owl.

Peace is in the present, moment after moment.

Chapter 12

She was greeting the day. Lea White Dove Lovesen is called to spread her truth. At a beautiful, adventurous human park, she gathers her students and other stylists from other internal movement systems. The house cat Jackie, join her while she is moving to a meditative music. The cat is sitting as they enjoy the cool breeze of the hypnotic day. Clear blue skies and the green lawn turf means, the time has come to seek the dance of internal energy balance. The vital connection of the five elements is the wisdom she has experienced daily.

Lea White Dove Lovesen creates and ravishes spirit in her physical body. Lea White Dove Lovesen is more than she appears. She is an old soul. "What are you wishing for people who study your lifestyle?" This is what becomes her call.

I wish for the way of love. The way grandmothers teach their grandkids to love and respect their Mom and Dad. As she receives the signal from spirit guides and teachers in her internal dance, an internal divine routine. To love externally means to respect others externally as well. No hitting others. No means no. A lesson in connecting to the root center is also called rooting. Lea White Dove Lovesen is a grandmother to several people. She teaches a style of internal consciousness.

Self-consciousness is consciousness that begins with the individual self. You are the most important person in your world. Without you, you don't have a world. The dance you are about to embark on begins inside your soul. This is self-awareness. Lea White Dove Lovesen is a "Peace Dancer" by her choice. She is alive, she is filled with unconditional love in all 9 centers of her core energy. The spinning of the 9 centers is a balancing of 9 aspects. The root center is balancing her true divine self with her material body connected to Great Mother Earth. This action is an internal divine dance. Regulated by her control of breath. Nature is calling to love the White Dove who is spinning and balancing daily. This is an ancient spiritual practice. Keeping well is the promise of Divine Order.

Lea White Dove Lovesen accepts her higher vibrational power animal. She is a White Dove. She dances daily healing those who see her as a divine healer. A person may or may not recognize the healer she is because of their perception of her. The task is a daily task. Like the thought waves of balancing is a task of "Peace Dancers". The dancers in 'Music, Movement, and Meditation" understands this insight well. Lea White Dove Lovesen was in the past trained very well by Luke Clear Eagle Lovesen. Now today she passes on the training with "Music, Movement, and Meditation". Pay close attention to the peace message of today.

Amma the dolphin holds energy for a long period to use and wards off energy deficiency at a later period in time. The same energy is stored in the atomic structure of our cells. This is the Great Mother energy lifestyle. Loving ways to their children as well as their grandchildren. A way of unconditional love. Balanced in breathing the wisdom and ways of divine dance. A baby dragon comes alive.

Chapter 13

A person stops the day of events and catches the teaching of the day. The music is a melodious sound in the background. They honor their brothers and sisters, taking time to understand the way of peace dances they are walking. Watching Lea White Dove Lovesen, they may not wish to meditate yet they meditate when they are thinking of not meditating. Defining meditation as an experience in touching personal enlightenment of an individual allows self-consciousness to grow. A dancer for World Peace is a dancer who is enlightened in the ways of self-love. Meditating on any theme they become enlightened. This is not a religious practice. You are the person to love. A "Peace Dancer" is deserving of all good things and one of the good things is love. Meow Now.

The Divine Child of the North is giving yourself the permission to heal in life and even awaken to all the essential positive possibilities of one hundred percent pure essential oils. While on your course, will someone you know or will someone you don't know touch the peaceful ways of media along with government to establish World Peace?

There are many paths to world peace. The question is, "How are we able to maintain peace?" Past teachers like "Master Cody Flying Eagle" and several teachers have taught Luke Clear Eagle Lovesen who shares with Lea White Dove Lovesen. Sharing the medicine of Amma the Dolphin and Sammy the Owl a breath of the divine, oneness is entwined. Today is a time for sharing peace and love experiences.

In your divine internal dance. What have you, dear peace, dancer learned about yourself? This question is about you, and your life experience to date. Your spiritual guide travels oceans and experiences nebulous physical truths imprinted on your body, mind, and emotions. Could it be possible to ask the question and get your answer? The answer may not have a sensation. Do "Peace Dancers" have sensations in their physical body? Has your mind cleared thoughts as you dance for world peace? The sensation of tears may have one wondering if they are loved.

The answer is to move out of the ego and dance to the clear zone of the spirit self. A consciousness of peace or a consciousness of love may heal late-stage injuries. Stay hydrated with pure filtered water during the dance workout.

Are you Lea White Dove Lovesen? Is your energy nurtured with spirit? All life knows spirit. Great Father Sky gives self-answers to dancers. Great Mother Earth allows the dancer a place to dance the "Baby Dragon" or the "Divine Child of the North" divine dances of internal peace. Not just physical slow dances of choice. "Divine Baby Dragon" and "Divine Child of the North" were created and taught by Luke Clear Eagle Lovesen.

Before the truth of transition, death appears to Master Cody Flying Eagle Templeton as a creative Martial Art Dances. Death is not the end of life, only a transcendence into spirit self, a truth, without a physical body.

With respect, Luke Clear Eagle a student of life. A creative internal ultimate energy dance as a tribute to life in peace. Today in this year, Luke Clear Eagle Lovesen along with Lea White Dove Lovesen share the energy of Grandmother Moon. Today, right now healing energy creates a rhythm of life. He opens the feminine side of himself.

Lea White Dove Lovesen opens her masculine side and protects her children and grandchildren. Observing the dolphins in the ocean, Amma the Dolphin introduces swimming, a way in which a new way of exercising and breathing in and with energy. Life is granted, dreams come true, and the ways of freedom is maintained.

Chapter 14

The way of Amma the Dolphin is a way of freedom, the same way found in the practice of being an Eagle. This is a spirit-self in energy. The movements of "Adolescents of the South". The controlled breath while Luke Clear Eagle Lovesen is reminded of the city of Atlantis. He was a true Atlantean. He is an eagle flying above the ocean. In the present time, he dances internally to the rhythm of music and his dream of world peace. Peace is a new spoken sound, within his dance. As an internal dance vibrates energy so does peace and manna. The energy of spirit is free and full of light. Luke Clear Eagle Lovesen dances as an "Adolescent of the South".

It is a dream come true for Amma the Dolphin to be receiving the Clear Golden White Yellow Light. She is awakened to the idea of speaking her truth. Lea White Dove Lovesen joins the "Divine Child of the North" internal energy balancing dance. The Great Star Nation is ablaze with intense energy dances in this new year, which is the year of the rabbit. Spirit consciousness opens the truth, the fact. Death is not the end. The end is the end. When a physical body is ended, the spirit of a warrior transcends. They become another light in the Rainbow of lights. Their soul is alive at a higher vibration and at another rhythm. This is a sound medicine. Frankincense is an assistant to wellness. There is no death, only transcendence for a warrior of Atlantis. There may even be a new transformation of the material body.

To learn a way of communication, a way of rhythm in the openness of sound warriors sing or chant. They may even play a musical instrument. Sooner or later every exterior dance is an internal dance and moves to an internal breath. A dance of controlled truism is controlled by the 3rd center breath work. Nothing is wrong. Though misinterpreted, the topic is correct because the "Peace Dancer" is a divine innovator. Clear is the color defining the physical, the color clear is not shaded. Clear accents the shade. The light of being clear is the universal divine light. All is clear. Lea White Dove Lovesen continues to *teach her the truth. Luke Clear Eagle Lovesen is her masculine energy inside her balanced with the feminine energy. When she faces her power source, her clockwise spin turns into a counterclockwise spin that moves from left to right when she faces her physical posterior.*

In other words, spinning masculine energy is creating feminine energy. As spinning feminine energy is also spinning the way of creating a counter to the masculine spinning of life. Balancing the two divine energy patterns is the answer to the question of "Why an internal dance style?" The lifestylist of Peace Dancers.

Chapter 15

Nitra-Girl Cat thanks Amma the Dolphin for her wisdom. The internal dances were created as a guide to the cellular healing process of the body and mind along with healing emotions. Meow Now! This has grown out from a new sea. Today is a good day for collecting "Peace Dancers". Teaching the way of protecting with shields to Nitra-Girl Cat. In his county field lesson is a way of setting boundaries. Focusing the way of an Armadillo, Astel is the energy of a boundary setter. You are the most important person in your world, without you, you don't have a world. Set boundaries, reset boundaries. Create a balance. Know your shields, Luke Clear Eagle Lovesen teaches that when a "Peace Dancer" breathes in, you may choose to breathe in an essential oil, assisting charismatic energy. Charming rosa damascena or Rose is a high energy for the heart of the "Peace Dancers". Every movement of the "Divine Ultimate Energy Dance" is balancing and powerful. "Meow Now" is Nitra-Girl Cat's song. Pulling up anchors is a job for Luke Clear Eagle Lovesen, creating an emotional armor, a shield for his emotional body that brings joy.

Breathing and moving are techniques. He was a "Peace Dancer" creating a flowing technique together from the power movement of pulling up anchors seeing Astel, the golden armadillo curled in a ball. The Peacer Dancer is raising his hands and arms to Grandfather Sky. He lowers the extremities, in a rhythm pulls his feet up together, then steps up forward. Astel the Armadillo is a boundary setter, teardrops symbolized by the wiggling of his fingers to the music of choice.

A question arises as "Peace Dancers" ground their dance in harmony. Each dancer in the dance of peace learns and practices physical movements to calm the emotions.

Am I calm while dancing the divine eight directional dance? Will Peace come if I am free from anxiety?

Boundaries are taught by Luke Clear Eagle Lovesen, Lea White Dove Lovesen, and various teacher levels. Established this year and carried on to the future years. This year is the time to shine. Setting freedom is a goal for Peace Dancers. The sunflower is a symbol in setting boundaries for freedom. The spirit self-consciousness means a "Peace Dancer" must create freedom as they dance the shields with light. Over Great Mother Earth, a rainbow of light from every other planet is projected, indicating each other's location in space and time. Clarity is a color in healing our social world.

This year is a chance to shine light on all humans as well as with animals and fish, because we are a hurting society. Water animals and birds alike enjoy the beauty of roses growing out of the earth. A herb and flower garden.

Astel the Armadillo will not cross boundaries since she is dancing the spiritual and mental program. Dear "Peace Dancers," this year is a new beginning for you to define your space because there are many who say that you haven't experienced it. The Golden White Yellow Light is your light, becomes the experience of rainbow light in the ultimate energy dance. In honor of World Peace this year, "Peace Dancers" are dancing the divine way on Great Mother Earth today. Congratulations to the internal warriors of the fair-spoken people this year. On the boundary of the home as a safe and protected place.

Astel the Armadillo offers her medicine and creates personal enjoyment within boundaries. Astel the Armadillo speaks to Nitra-Girl Cat and creates greatness. Nitra-Girl Cat is telling the "Peace Dancers" to be the Internal Dancer they are now. "Why Meow?" she says to all "Peace Dancers" of the universe. Generally speaking, all cats are peaceful; they are merely food-hungry and hunters. Since it is open and free when they are outside their boundaries, they all remain inside them. Established freedom in 50 states. "Meow" for the free United States of America. Setting the United States to be free. Meow to be free of vaccine medicine, free for home pets and humans. The "Mask of Meow". Soft-spoken and even sleeping in a curled position as Astel the Armadillo taught her children to set uncropped boundaries.

Nitra-Girl Cat said, "Meow Now," to Luke Clear Eagle Lovesen, Lea White Dove Lovesen, and to their Ultimate Internal Dance for World Peace.

The focused attention of some "Peace Dancers" is yet to establish an internal self-consciousness of boundary setting. On January 12, this year—the year of the rabbit—a beautiful dance in eight directions was performed with the intention of bringing joy within.

Chapter 16

"Meow Now". This is why I'm upset, hissed Nitra-Girl Cat. A house cat living the life of a bus station cat. It's time to get off the bus, Nitra-Girl Cat said, "Meow Now," establishing both healthy bounds and uncropped free borders. Nitra-Girl Cat began a new bath. Today, Astel the Armadillo is a boundary-setting leader. In herself, she finds personal joy. While the war in other countries became alive, war never worked and caused a lot of money. House Cats may feel a bit that they are being used. Their pride is in the hunting state, catching mice and rabbits, keeping disease and infection down. Sending a warning frequency to the workout and dance area, along with other household cats.

Lea White Dove Lovesen builds her Golden White Yellow Light between the palms of her hand. She sends golden white energy out from herself, as she enters back into the core of her material form. Lea White Dove Lovesen now is freeing the stagnant energy. This action is freeing the dimming of this light as she begins waving her hands like clouds. A wave of hands like clouds is the internal action giving her aura of Golden White Yellow Light. As she starts to render richer blood, her core moves and becomes less cloudy. Lea White Dove Lovesen began to look and feel younger and brighter. As she feels younger and brighter, she looks even more younger and brighter. This is positive control of her natural light, her unconditional love towards herself. Focusing on Golden White Yellow Light is a way of life, under and in front of the "Tree of Life". Lea White Dove Lovesen is building a safe red center. "Meow Now" is spoken by Jackie-Girl Cat and Nitra-Girl Cat in protection and as well in Golden White Yellow Light.

A boundary-setting house cat energy is sent to her root center, red in color, and creates a new healing self. Today she watches Lea White Dove Lovesen use music with slow movement. She dances with the "Divine Child of the North", the internal prayer dance well inside herself, her core. Her root center connects the female and male positive energy inside of herself.

Her divine energy is shared with the inner child in the balancing of their core and becomes her core as she comes to life with the self-consciousness of her beautiful divine self. Then she connects her core to the creative self. Lea White Dove Lovesen is awakened to her feminine nature where she ignites her positive loving light. Strengthened by her love, the light of the "Goddess" is her divine self. As in a divine ultimate energy dance. She is moved by her divine self.

Astel the Armadillo is setting up her shield of truth. Lea White Dove Lovesen is really eager to understand the lesson of establishing boundaries. She goes to practice a peace dance the way of Astel the Armadillo, the boundary setter, who speaks a way of honoring personal enjoyment. Lea White Dove Lovesen becomes a boundary of golden white yellow light.

Astel the Armadillo praises this internal energy dance. The "Divine Child of the North" is growing from frustration by design. Children of physical consciousness grow in this year. Internal Dance skills are for wellness and health benefits. The human immune system becomes alive. Turning the core of an internal life energy system the goosebumps become alive indicating a strong immune system. Breathing in pure, 100% essential peppermint oil while bending your knees and extending your arms back and forth. Lea White Dove Lovesen is the greatest; she offers healing hands. She becomes conscious of her core. A physical body is housing her spiritual self. Following her natural movements, she exhales toxins such as carbon dioxide and breathes in oxygen. She is also reminded to clear her thoughts to have a clear light energy.

She turns to her core and she sees herself inside. She shifts her weight to her front side, bending and bringing her elbows down. She finally steps a left-foot forward energy dance step and presses her left palm with the knife edge of her right hand. She examines her core center within to make sure all nine centers are balanced. She feels the power of being balanced. Connected to Great Mother Earth, she is rooted in her life *energy. Today top soil energy comes to her. Every peace dancer shares Great Mother Earth ground power at the first center, red in color, located at the base of her spine. Chanting the sound "Lam" now, Lea White Dove Lovesen opens a practice of safety. Practicing the boundary-setting becomes the Golden White Yellow Light within her pelvic core. Her physical center is red as she breathes in, and she accepts her root center. Her spirit self is grounded in her hips. "Ah, Ho" is chanted many times.*

Her internal energetic dance becomes alive, as lush self-pleasure becomes created at her uterus level. She chants the sound of "Lam". A self-protection power light of red rises from her roots. As this clear red light rises, it changes to the color orange. The divine light is filling her genital area with love-inspiring light.

Chapter 17

The creation of a harmonious balance connects the sacred self to others. As with "MMM" the healing of deep cell memories is self-loving therapy of the "DNA" in the cell. Lea White Dove Lovesen repeated aloud, "Meow Now," as Nitra-Girl Cat and Jackie-Girl Cat said it.

Be aware of being treated like a clown in a circus that possibly could be opening up to the clown in the local cat.

"Meow now".

Nitra-Girl Cat and Jackie-Girl Cat join the local "Peace Dancers". The park now has become a hosting place for students of ultimate personal power. She hears the music and feels loving energy in every movement. Rainbow light begins with a harmonious monument of ultimate power; her internal center "Vam" creates a new life of an inspired being. "Vam" is kept in either the taker or a close companion. "Peace Dancers" work with creative emotions in every dance where the teachings of the ways of internal movement.

People become personally joyous when Nitra-Girl Cat sits because her ultimate bliss is turned on. Joy signs into the aura of the sensual world. She is at her right side approximately six feet from her energized physical body. This is an energy practice. The art of setting up boundaries. The art of protecting the genital area. "Meow Now" calls Nitra-Girl Cat and Jackie-Girl Cat out to divinely dance with Lea White Dove Lovesen. The power of masculine energy shines red light on as well as inside the root core of a beautiful athletic dancer. She returns the Coos to Nitra-Girl Cat, who is fluffy and her needs are met.

Luke Clear Eagle Lovesen joins the energy of today. The concept of COVID and 23 fake diseases are not brought up at the dance; instead, the "Sarasota Cat Club for World Peace" was established to put a stop to the war. Why is it advertised as Covid 19 in this divine life year? Humans are loving and inspired to "Meow without a mask"! Nitra-Girl Cat heard she was a mere cat and got confused. As she was confused she *wondered, "Why Meow?" "Will humans understand that the cats cannot wear a mask as they hunt mice?"*

Lea White Dove Lovesen thanks Jackie-Girl Cat and the Sarasota Cat Club. Nitra-Girl Cat meows back to all Peace Dancers of today. Lea White Dove Lovesen is a present-day great researcher as she became a sounding board for the lake "Council of Cats". This council becomes open. Along with Luke Clear Eagle Lovesen, he organizes a meeting of "Peace Dancers," including the "8 Directions Peace Prayer Dance" at dusk and a peace dance at dawn. A moving external meditation is seen from an internal view. These centers house a song for Lea White Dove Lovesen as joined with Luke Clear Eagle Lovesen creating a pair of Lovesens. A musical song vibrates to sounds heard by harp, tenor flute, and various wind and string musical instruments.

Chapter 18

In the new world, peace opens when facing the south-east direction. Nitra-Girl Cat came out from the bush in the front area of the garden to witness the plans of protection in place at the base of Luke Clear Eagle Lovesen. This is her statement. Luke Clear Eagle Lovesen spoke to Nitra-Girl Cat in Meow language, his first ever Mountain Lion wisdom that was given to him at the "Sarasota Council of Cats" and presented to Nitra-Girl Cat.

The foundation of harmony is compassion; with the grace of Great Mother Earth, we are able to survive. One dance may be joined by others asking the question "What worked in a time of masculine energy that creates safety and protection for all divine peace dancers?" Nitra-Girl Cat can see the answer to world peace in the 8 principles of leadership. Nitra-Girl Cat paused at the noisy mobile couch of the delivery system.

Nitra-Girl Cat shook her head and licked her chops as she pulled herself together to run if she needed to. She paused and explored with her keen eyes. The light of a Mountain Lioness saw a sleek female form sitting in a southeast direction. The color of Golden White Yellow Light didn't express harm to anyone. Mountain Lioness is the root of the blessings of lessons in survival. Camel the Mountain Lioness opens the leadership medicine for a troubled and traumatized society. Her roaring was saying to Lea White Dove Lovesen that the way of the masculine past didn't work for wellness in a warring society. Take the children and run to the other world on the other end of the lake.

Covid-19 is of the past trying to get you Nitra-Girl Cat to wear a Mask. "The light of the rainbow shines internally", said Luke Clear Eagle Lovesen. He began chanting "Om Mani Pademe Hung", the chant of compassion as he plays his flute with clear notes. He played a love song created for the power of the Mountain Lion. The power of the Mountain Lion energy comes alive inside of Lea White Dove Lovesen. Luke Clear Eagle Lovesen is expressing his feminine roots in his roots. He continues to dance the "Divine Child of the North" facing the southeast direction while he is creating a calm composure. He is sending calm composure to Lea White Dove Lovesen. Nitra-Girl Cat senses as she allows a wave of compassion to protect her and lays down again. The nine physical centers of the body are balanced by eight principles that make up feminine leadership.

Lea White Dove Lovesen balances herself daily to be able to join the power animal, Camel the Mountain Lioness. Her leadership is the wisdom found in all-natural and domestic cats. The wonder of how Lea White Dove Lovesen becomes the marked object for others to point a finger and blame has been solved.

Large cats are marked with misinterpretation. Our public along with private school systems are expressing a way of leadership this year. The school needs the soul of the Mountain Lioness to roar today, a Roar without any misunderstanding. Human people need a roar now to hear the call leaders of today. Wake up, to meet their needs. "Meow Now" says Nitra-Girl Cat and Jackie-Girl Cat.

"Roar" said Camel the Mountain Lioness in reply. The interruption of their divine soul dance causes Luke Clear Eagle Lovesen and Lea White Dove Lovesen to pause in respect. The message from the great soul of leadership is not taken in the wrong way today. An art to guide schools with a way to dance in ultimate movement power as a person is dancing internally. The power in our United States is in the freedom of public schools. Other and all Mountain Lioness leaders are the medicine for insecurities. Know yourself, powerful peacemakers. The energy for remembering the 8 divine internal dances is deficient. Numerous schools, communities, and states in the US are no longer free. Teens stay at home and study while their parents work from home because they are terrified to go to school.

You are asked to open the energy of the hunter and resume the Divine Dance. "Okay" said Luke Clear Eagle Lovesen and Lea White Dove Lovesen. This "Divine Dance Adolescent of the South" led with the courage found in the heart of their center.

The foreknowledge is in 2023 teaching the ways of breathing. Life is divine, a support system shimmering a Golden White Yellow Light. This is a real dance. A base of prayer in every dance.

Chapter 19

The power of shimmering lights gathers at the base of Nitra-Girl Cat she is presenting a message that in this year, parents are being instructed to find ways to teach peace to the school children. A constant challenge in going to school. Guns are a thought of being superior in school and are a way of daily training. "Do as I tell you", is the command of the Gun person "or I will shoot you." This power is nothing but a false power. The reason typical schools have lesser attendance is because of the shooting of parents, grandparents, and other adults in addition to other teenagers.

Lea White Dove Lovesen asks the question to all who may hear it. "Do those working in the educational system intend to teach students about proper behavior in the classroom?" The press reported that a teenager assisted in his mother's rescue during a cleanup period. After the teenager, Hank, shot his grandmother for yelling at his mother, he was eventually taken into custody and placed in jail.

Camel the Mountain Lioness looks into the eyes of Lea White Dove Lovesen. A mind connection is a process of keeping the peace as wisdom grows intellectually. "Peace Dancers" practice the art of letting go as they understand deeply inside the third eye center. There is only a sense of ease and no longer any fear when dancing as a "Divine Child of the North."

Teens and school children support Hank, who acted ignorantly. He thought he was controlling the frantic grandmother in the trigger-pulling incident. Was his mother not in need of safety? Camel the Mountain Lioness roared loudly and Hank was in the good right. Protecting the mother. When the power sound dissipated, peace was again witnessed.

A teenager Hank owned a handgun for protection. Yet without proper education, he didn't know what to do and the world lost a "Grandmother". His mother went into a diabetic coma in the "Yankee Street Medical Center" while he is in prison. After consulting with Hank, Dr. Bernie Tomlin, the psychology counselor, learned that Hank acted in the best way possible during a difficult period. The only way to find out is to speak with his mother once she awakens from her coma. The police released Hank to the custody of the home to take care of the domestic needs of the house cats.

Chapter 20

Hank Tompson is a teenager. After driving there for the past two days to check in, he left his 45-caliber pistol at the police station. After that, he proceeded to the hospital where his mother was being treated by doctors to check on her recovery from her "Diabetic Coma." He needed daily counseling as to what to do. His Grandmother was at the cremation society and scheduled for cremation. He took responsibility for domestic needs; his father Tom didn't live at home and was not married to Anne any longer. When he asked his dad to contact him, his father wanted to avoid the responsibility.

Hank Tompson looked into the eyes of the police officer. "You are wise to come as instructed" said Officer Niles. "It appears your mother Anne has recovered and was informed of what has happened." Hank is speechless and remains silent.

He was in his own custody at home to take care of the house and four-legged cat. He had to check in daily at the Police Station to report his whereabouts, visit the hospital and follow the after-death plans of cremation. Once the court decides on the truth of his actions. No, he couldn't just go into hiding, he had to face the Judge of the Court and get a ruling as to what his future would be. How long his mother Anne Tompson was to stay in a diabetic coma? She was supposed to have the last say in how the judge and court made decisions.

A Mountain Lioness shadow was with Hank Tompson wherever he went. After losing Hank's grandfather, his father, and his grandmother as well as his Mother who's currently in a coma state, who indeed was all he wished to protect. Anne was in an anxiety state and he wished peace and healing for her. "Hank, you need to share your dreams," said Anne. "Look deep into my eyes that once were closed and today are awake. My eyes are open, my diet and insulin levels are balanced and I'm awake and conscious of my son's struggle. I looked for you as you looked for me. The time has come, the time is now to review our purpose together.

As Hank and Anne give each other hugs in front of their lawyer, soft jazz music fills the space. Essential oils of sage, and geranium, orange, rose lavender, and spruce fills a person's senses with a refreshing smell in the room. As their power animal shares the wisdom of vital senses as they release negative memories. The smell of Citrus sinensis and orange will help a two-legged person to get rid of the mind of depression.

Laughter is a sound practice in the movements of Lea White Dove Lovesen. She breathed in and allows the essential oil to create more laughter. After three minutes of high-quality laughter, Hank and Anne Tompson began a new life.

Chapter 21

A Pathfinder is walking with intent on a misty sunny day in Sarasota Florida. Luke Clear Eagle Lovesen is watching Nitra-Girl Cat crouch and hide in the bushes of protection. The leadership message was made to the "Peace Dancers" of this year. Luke Clear Eagle Lovesen was unable to rouse Nitra-Girl Cat from the brush because she had sensed Mel the Wolf's energy, which appeared and reminded peace dancers of their self-awareness. Nitra-Girl Cat continued the expression of light as a protecting, soul light of Luke Clear Eagle Lovesen.

Today, wild nature brought out the natural teacher in all people who turned to nature for the next lesson on how to walk on a harmonious peaceful path. Mel the Wolf instills a sense of family and loyalty. A clan of ultimate energy dancers form an internal dance with nature. Mel the Wolf's lesson today is well-rounded. Peace is a pathway to living. Regarding health is a daily internal dance. Singing for American Freedom is a song chanted with a connection to the internal spirit returning to the Divine Dance of self-love. Breathing life is a motivation for life as taught in the ancient ways of peacemakers. Studying the secrets of life, a text of Guru Howi Cansar. "Did the wolf create the human family or the human family copy the ways of the wolf medicine, as a resource to peace could be life without conflict and emotional pain?" is the last question he leaves unanswered.

Finding internal spiritual resources is a key to unlocking the internal programs for peace and self-love. Practice every 4–12 hours as part of your daily maintenance. Practice MMM or internal Tai Chi Dancing one to two times a day or whenever a "Peace Dancer" finds peace dance is necessary. Without being told what to do a "Peace Dancer" has already found the cellular DNA level of peace. Self-awareness becomes consciousness. This consciousness shifts with a degree of ease as a trance becomes induced.

Dear people, it is your choice to find peace in your life. Master Teacher Luke Clear Eagle Lovesen and Lea White Dove

Lovesen dance a path of self-love. Letting go of the negative emotions is in the "Divine Child of the North" dance. People walk by the dancers for peace. Daily they are healed and set free in a family way. Letting go of chemical warfare as promised in the late 1960s during the hippie era. Drew the Wolf is one of the "Peace Dancers". His Divine Child of the North was rediscovered this year, a time when there may be people who don't wish for freedom. The chemical war was re-activated in 2022. Practiced now. Time to let go. Go inside and become free.

Chapter 22

The wave begins as the ocean draws the current. Saltwater buildup and raises up to the heavens or Great Father Sky. When it peaks, it curls forming a white color in the peak. When the peak breaks, it crashes back on itself. Gravity brings saltwater waves back to Mother Earth, the beach is flooded. The natural balance is repeated again and again. Luke Clear Eagle Lovesen raised and opened his hands. He becomes his mental self where thoughts are stored and raised. He has the power to open and close positive thoughts. He gathers the universal positive brainwave energy of his creative personal medicine given to him by Drew the Wolf. This ultimate power dance is balancing with his breath. The energy of Mother Nature is opened and the medicine of the ocean is a life-giving medicine shared by Drew the Wolf, a teacher of life, a oneness with the way of love. Great truth may be a large knowledge to take at once. Therefore, the Divine Dance is practiced with large, deep breaths, and slow long movements. Becoming humble is to attain new heights. The consciousness belonging to your spirit guide and teacher is in the enlightenment of each movement. Starlight is the "Peace Dancer's" true self. Drew the Wolf is one of the most powerful "Peace Dancers". Howl as Luke Clear Eagle Lovesen gathers the energy of Drew the Wolf. He feels the freedom to let go of emotional troubles.

He feels a sensation of relaxation like a wave of brainwave activity coming over him as he senses. His eye muscles relax as he closes his eyes. He practices the sound and art of howling. Hearing the sound of letting go is relaxing the jaws of his face. Relating to his calming relaxed state of consciousness, his jaw muscles also relax. He enters a higher vibrational state of calmness. He allows his physical body to better the immune system and improves blood circulation. He is taking time in balancing the triple warmer energy channel.

He did not know if he was in a trance state of self-loving. Healing diseases. He asked himself was his emotional anxiety a level of self-attack? Creating a limited view. Drew the Wolf makes a howling noise and advises releasing any "Self-Attacks." These self-attacks don't benefit any "Peace Dancer" and aren't self-fulfilling. Thus, let it go and release it. Courage to do this is a lesson in Camel the Mountain Lioness teachings. The inner cave dwellers have found Camel the Mountain Lioness was found on cave walls all over the world. Lessons of longevity and self-healing are found on cave walls and clay pots. One of those lesson is from Camel the Mountain Lioness who taught life is about growing. Growth is achieved when the "Peace Dancer" releases and let go of harmful stagnation. Nitra-Girl Cat passes these lessons to Luke Clear Eagle Lovesen. Perhaps these are harmful emotions held for years and years.

Self-expression is howling. Howling is the expression found in the moon's vibrational energy. Full moon days are the ideal time to howl at the moon. Meow Now.

Release, let go of negative emotions as the "Divine Child of the North" allows growth for our hearts to hold one another in the positive spirit.

Chapter 23

"Meow Now" is joined by the howling of Camel the Mountain Lioness and Drew the 4 legged Wolf people who are alive in the Manatee County of Florida this hot summer day in June this year. Asking the Manatee Schoolboard to take a good long look at the schools of Sarasota now and the future of schools in Sarasota and other towns and cities. The schools of Florida need to ask, "What are students and teachers and other places of gathering learning? What do we advocate for a positive newscast at night?" Howling just across and down Phillippi creek happens in June this year. Knowing is what your children learned in a human trafficking and gun-driven society of disrespectful humans "Meow Now" as you listen to your call as Jupiter and Saturn in the heavens on the Great Mother Earth in the Bay Front Park and Atlantean Ocean create a world of governments gone egotistical. Displaying a very Leo "Meow Now".

"Is this what peace cultures want? Is a better leadership sharing dances of understanding peace and the causes of peace a shared program?" Nitra-Girl Cat passed a "Peace Dancers" of the pool of water dance bring the "Divine Swimming Baby Dragon", "Divine Swimming Child of the North" and "Divine Adolescent of the South" a new way of old ways of retreating within connecting in spirit medicine as they become a new guide of the lessons of "No Death Only Transcendence", a lesson of howling. Use the lessons and teachings to learn that humans have four bodies.

Every person may be a Land Rock or Water Dancer under Great Father Sky on Father's Day sharing a physical body in the dance of "Ra" energy. Their mental body is inspired by the ways of truth and respect in the school system they attend. In June this year, they are in need to take information about their behaviors as they "Meow Now" or howl to heal and release stagnated energy blocking the Golden White Yellow Light of Lord Jesus and "Ra" energy of 10 Commandments. "Meow

Now" is the sounds of life "No Death Only Transcendence" anchoring a program of peace "Meow now".

Big cats have taught the Roar for Life with the howling of Drew the Wolf guide teaching. Respect is a value that must be instilled, according to Drew the Wolf, who is leading the Board of Teachers. Howling is a way to respect "Peace Dancers" letting them know the wolf is present. And "Peace Dancers" learn to respect the wolf bringing the lessons and a "Song of the Wolf" awakening a better teachers and schools. Teaching music and the "Joy of Song" honoring the values of great teachers of the past who taught the ways of the past and the future song creation of the new "Peace Dancer" dancing to internal trace music awakening the soul consciousness in public schools.

Drew the Wolf (howls) to the center of Great Mother Earth. To the soil, rock, and water. This is a good time to balance the nine energy centers of a person's core. As they seek refuge in the miracles of life as "Peace Dancers" they truly are. This song and dance of life is not being taught in private or public schools personally. So it is time to (howl) to Great Father Sky. The universal space in time this year. Drew the Wolf learns the truth he can count on. This truth will not be taken away from him because it is a part of him.

This is a "Peace Dancer's" song and dance or universal love and creation of world peace. Camel the Mountain Lioness and Drew the Wolf open the howling session. World Peace this year is your lifestyle .

Chapter 24

Howling, singing, or chanting a song is music. This is a way to know the truth of what we have learned. Experience is a way of an external or internal dance of the "Peace Dancers". World peace daily as they justify their actions in movement and meditation to a society. Drew the Wolf presents an answer to the question. "What do you want, oh confused Peace Dancers?" Grounding with shade of red roots. Moving with controlled breathing. Finding a calming space internally and a quiet place externally. Visualize red roots connecting to the network of soil, rock, and water. Connecting to the core of Great Mother Earth. Meow Now.

Creating what you want in peace for a healing with Great Mother Earth. The Great Mother Earth's core is spinning. Stimulating a spinning in the root center at the base of the spine in the center of the hips. Luke Clear Eagle Lovesen and Lea White Dove Lovesen share a red energy light grounding deep inside themselves. Rooting peace they evolve into a Golden White Yellow Light as they awaken to the calling of 8 directions deep inside themselves.

Maintaining this awakening of world peace, Nitra-Girl Cat and Jackie-Girl Cat say "Meow Now" which protects Great Mother Earth with clear Golden White Yellow Light, spinning in the core of their root center. The harbinger is in the spinning core in the MMM dance and in the Divine Person Dance. A new life is created with a swimming Divine Baby Dragon Dance in the tropical waters of Florida therapeutic pools. Jackie-Girl Cat is licking her paw now.

What do we want for our future society to look like? Drew the Wolf brings the Wolf Medicine of howling to the public and private school systems, and special school systems. To work this summer in the heat and humidity.

Knowing that the tropical storms in Florida are passing by Sarasota as the wolf reminds the children to stay hydrated, have less sugar in their diet and eat proteins. Are you having trouble digesting, eating digestive enzymes, and making sure in the (howling) you drink clean filtered and pure water? Watch out for phony water that is inexpensive or even free to consume carelessly at establishments.

Drew the Wolf howls the message to the children. Drew the Wolf reminded the children to stay hydrated. You are the most important person in your world. Long continuous howling awakens the hunter's instinct. You cannot have a world without you.

Beware of tornadoes as well as lightning and thunderstorms. As soon as you hear the thunder, stop your activity and change your thoughts. Drink more filtered water. That is cool, if not cold to a "Peace Dancer".

The rain in a tropical storm brings a new life as it cools Great Mother Earth. Her soil holds and regulates the flood. The water element is controlled by truth, rock people, and soil people.

The water element along with the Great Water Goddess bring life to the kidney's energy. More energy is brought to the water bladder. When the water bladder is full, the physical body dances. Walks even run for relief. Fear is letting go of toxic fluids. Howling is a state of consciousness as it occurs. This is a natural process in the physical animal. This is okay to realize the water as you dance on in dreamtime people of the planet. Letting go of your fears is what a great pro does. Begin with visualizing your root center. Chanting the sound of red, a low steady vibration at the Root Center of the Golden White Yellow Light of your spirit becomes balanced with red lights that are balanced. The rain cleanses the material body. Rain light is clear and clean. Howling is an exercise in loving oneself. Nitra-Girl Cat stops licking her paw to ease her right front paw and listens to Drew the Wolf howling to her class.

Howling stimulates the thinking and brainwave patterns of the "Peace Dance" "Meow Now", roaring in delight. Howling, roaring, the horse whining, and the bird singing. Nature is a whale or dolphin singing its song, a balanced water electromagnetic vibration is in the song of your power self. "Meow Now" is Nitra-Girl Cat in tune with a harmonious night or day. "Peace Dancers" balance the energy of the kidney, water bladder system, and meridians. It is shown to aid in the recovery of broken bones as well as related injuries. A balanced water element is strong bones yet bones not overgrown or brittle. "Meow Now" says Nitra-Girl Cat and Jackie-Girl Cat. Do it today. "Meow Now".

Chant: The classic "Om tategatagata om. Bergase, bergase maha. Bergase, bergase rasa. Sume gata sume gata soha". Awakening the Wolf medicine mind, we are learning how to heal with our energy and spirit self.

Sixty-four wolves were howling at the shores of Phillippi Creek and the lakes of the subdivision and Siesta Key this year. "Peace Dancers" become freedom pathfinders singing and dancing under the Full Moon on 12th of January. This lesson is from Drew the Wolf when he is teaching the children what they need to know. The colon is cleansed and refined colon related illnesses are soothed. Nitra-Girl Cat lived up to her given name. She scratched as she covered up the not so smelly sample. A "Meow Now" balances the water and wood elements.

"Peace Dancers" of the world, internal and external worlds of themselves, dance the divine developmental stage of internal and external peace dance. A Hummingbird appears on the green lawn. Your calling has arrived. Hummingbirds are small birds outside exposing the joy for internal ultimate energy as their food for life. When this dance is taught properly as Luke Clear Eagle Lovesen and Lea White Dove Lovesen teach. The "Divine Child of the North" dances a sacred internal "Dance of Joy" helping in the clean-up of Great Mother Earth. Knowing "Joy" is when a Musical, Movement, and Meditation is implied.

Chapter 25

A "Joy" dance on the green and pool areas around Sarasota Florida. Focusing on their soul, the "Peace Dancer" may find a feeling of pure happiness in internal and external dance. This is shown as the "Peace Dancer" dances. This is a medicine that prehistoric humans used on a daily basis. This is the medicine to help in solving pain, diseases, and problems of the mind. Assist in converting and dissolving our adversity into something more positive. That's the Joy of the Dance. Joy the Hummingbird reaches out in 8 directions. Nitra-Girl Cat sits on the path as cats often do basking in the shadows as she listens to Joy the Hummingbird. These are lessons on joy as healing the families of humans. The "Peace Dancer" is alive and awakened.

Love as well as peace charms are used on this day of joy. MMM necklaces are used to create a sense of joy during their daily divine peace day dance in eight directions. Today, Joy the Hummingbird brings personal teachings. Nitra-Girl Cat meows in the southeast direction to begin with the love of life together as the lovesens do with their relationship. The experience and expression of love is joy. Moving comfortably, to dance as one in a beautiful environment. A taste of the emotional body of peace is experienced when one helps others to succeed in experiencing the joy of life. Not to be practiced unless the dancer wants peace. During the time of conflicts, peacetime is shown to be created. Enough "Peace Dancers" are dancing MMM or Tai Chi style dances with related style dance prayer. Peace Dances help in stopping aggressions of war and conflict. Blaming other people and other countries is not an answer to the conflicts. Smiling is a result of the empty way Divine Peace Dance. Whatever style of the dance, it brings a smile on the face of the peace dancer. It helps to stop the conflicts in Ukraine and Syria, Middle East, Russia and China. Decide to save lives and stop the possible war.

In World War III, "Meow Now".

Camel the Mountain Lioness teaches ways of peace to Nitra-Girl Cat and Jackie-Girl Cat. "Peace Dancers" dance holding an energy shield of joy. Smile is the answer. Laughing is an answer to opening the peace actions in the government. As a Peace Dancer, you became one of the creators who gave many gifts during the trying times. Hummingbird reminds us to dance, and Peace Dancers begin to smile.

Chapter 26

Your purpose has a meaning that is clearer to the "Peace Dancer". When you bring your right and left hands over your heart center, you are creating an essential oil dance for balance along the peace path daily. The meaning is now her story.

Sometimes dance in Sarasota Florida, Seattle Washington, Santa Fe New Mexico, Green Mountain Vermont, and other peace conscious gatherings where peace is created every day throughout the day.

Begin with gathering the nine energy centers. Balance each center in harmony which day and night holds a golden white yellow light. The light of each of these meowed centers are being practiced where it begins spinning as well as form the centers. Balancing these nine centers internally, a "Peace Dancer" becomes more and more conscious and aware.

Begin with the first center at the base of the spine, the light is golden, white, and yellow. The lights are dancing in this center of the source, connecting to the bedrock of the soul, your source in the human physical body. Allow your mind to gather a sense of balance. Meow is the tool for who you are. The divine light is red in color and you dance an internal passion, a dance of your ancestors. Listen to sacred trance music of flute and song.

Great Mother Earth is transmitting positive energy through "Peace Dancers" as she allows you and even invites you to share peace. As you send red roots to her, you are the Golden White Yellow Light you see in the red roots. Your root center is clearer. You share joy as an essential oil for emotion. Dancing is releasing harmful disease producing energy causing stagnation and weakening your first center effects. A "Peace Dancer" may feel the grounding balance in life. The Red Root Center light is spinning golden, white, yellow light. No stagnation of energy. The Golden White Yellow Light is your Divine self, positive by nature. It becomes brighter like the sun of a natural sky. You become brighter and rise from your roots at your feet. You enter the second centre that is located in the middle of hips and sacrum.

While this center is often not treated with respect, this center is orange in color and used in creation of positive life. "Peace Dancers are born in the month of October. Peace Dancers will share the creation of life in society. Balance the sexual center and create a positive energy light of orange spinning with the feminine and masculine love. Creating new life as the orange light in darkness. "Meow Now" even the Howl of a lone wolf in your divine self. As you dance, you see the orange and clear light spinning in the creation center of the hips above the red light. Make love as you dance for world peace . "Meow Now" as you dance says Nitra- Girl Cat and Jackie Girl Cat. They lay down and licks their paws in the heat of June. The Divine Golden White Yellow Light spins and is stronger in this orange light. "Meow Now " dances in Joy. Balancing the hips on and or in water dance programs are necessary.

How does a peace dancer know their internal light is balanced? Great Nitra-Girl Cat is often asked. She Looks into Luke Clear Eagle Lovesen's eyes. She sees a Great Golden White Yellow Light brightly at his second creation center.

As the divine inside himself is alive and growing, the power of the light is shared with Lea White Dove Lovesen and in the system of life where a light is conceived. Peace and love are united with life creating a light producing energy golden and white in color and becomes the peace and love is dance everywhere. This light is for peace on a world level. On the physical level, a "Peace Dancer " becomes the lights of gold, white, and yellow shining light. The energy awakens the third light center at the solar plexus center. We dance and digest life. Meowing is a call to feed the cats. A two-legged person may not know when to stop for food. Food for their tummy. Good stopping point. Feed the tummy. Nitra-Girl Cat calls out the cry of a hungry tummy. "Meow" long loud sound, "Now" short softer sound and she sits. She begins licking her paws and preparing for a meal at six o'clock pm, post summertime sacred internal dance workout. The day was cloudy and low *in heaven pressure close to Great Father Sky. "Meow-Now" "Peace Dancers" dances in harmony with a sense of peace and love.*

"Meow Now"

On the remaining 6 centers of the sacred dancing hands dance in 8 directions following a feeding of Nitra-Girl Cat and Jackie-Girl Cat.

Her full stomach is enhanced with energy from the essential oil of peppermint,(Mentha piperita) in the air around the "Peace Dancer". Just sharing the air of a "Peace Dancer" is opening a way to life-enhancing connotation of the "Peace Dancer". Gifting the dancer of peace with the fragrance of 100% pure essential oils meow a possibility that peppermint essential oil is Menthol, Menthone, Menthonefurance. Cineole, also known as Eucalyptol, another gift from the creator is labeled as Pulegone along with Methyl Acetate. Could the Marseilles people have used peppermint essential oil in their cooking, traveling, and in their "Peace Dances"?

"Meow Now" states Nitra-Girl Cat is a house cat of leadership in schools and in power. Moving the core of Golden White Yellow Light of the Heart center, "Peace Dancers" share a green in color light as they continue their dance of love. Focus the mind on clear light free from harmful bacteria, any anti-moral or parasitic beings which block the Golden White Yellow Light self. "Meow Now" seeing the Golden White Yellow Light in their aura of spirit light the "Peace Dancer" is working to wellness and perfect health. So they also chant "Meow Now". A long deep controlled breath is a way of life dancing internally. "Meow Now" working on the fifth center located in the upper chest of a "Peace Dancer". "Meow" is the thoughts and a strong immune center, the answer for controlling diseases and imbalances.

In four bodies of Golden White Yellow Light. The immune center is life in harmony with life. Peppermint enhances air quality and is a vital life force in a drop. Don't dance the life *force way unless you want to have a strong immune defense. "Meow Now" says Nitra-Girl Cat.*

www.ingramcontent.com/pod-product-compliance
Lightning Source LLC
LaVergne TN
LVHW010609070526
838199LV00063BA/5117